# Can You Make Me Better?

This title has been published with the co-operation of Cherrytree Books
Amicus Illustrated is published by Amicus
P.O. Box 1329, Mankato, Minnesota 56002

Printed in Mankato, Minnesota, USA by CG Book Printers, a division of
Corporate Graphics

Library of Congress Cataloging-in-Publication Data

Bode, Ann de.
 Can you make me better? / Ann de Bode.
    p. cm. -- (Side by side)
 Summary: Rosie goes to the hospital to have surgery on her heart, then spends
time there getting better.
 ISBN 978-1-60753-178-4 (library binding)
[1. Medical care--Fiction. 2. Hospitals--Fiction. 3. Heart--Surgery--Fiction.]  I.
Title.
 PZ7.B633618Can 2012
 [E]--dc22
                                       2011002240

13-digit ISBN:  978-1-60753-178-4  First Edition 1110987654321
This edition © Evans Brothers Limited 2011
2A Portman Mansions, Chiltern Street, London W1U 6NR, United Kingdom

© Van In, Lier, 1995. Van In Publishers, Grote Markt 39, 2500 Lier, Belgium
Originally published in Belgium as Mag het licht nog even ann?

Rosie has a bad heart.
The doctor will make it better.
"We'll look after you in the hospital, Rosie.
Bring your favorite toys with you."

3

Rosie packs her bag —
books, games, crayons, and Teddy.
"Stay close to me, Teddy," she says.
"And don't worry. I'll soon feel better."

Rosie tries on her new pajamas.
Teddy has new pajamas, too,
and a little nightcap to match.

"I like my big bed," says Rosie,
at the hospital.
"Look, Teddy, it has wheels.
We can go for a ride!"

6

Rosie's mom stays in the hospital with Rosie.
But her bed is not really big enough!

The nurse puts a needle into Rosie's
arm to take a little blood.
Rosie tries to be brave, but she
feels scared, and cries a bit.

"You're being very brave, Rosie," says the nurse.
"Would you like to choose some
toys to play with?"
Rosie dives into a big box.

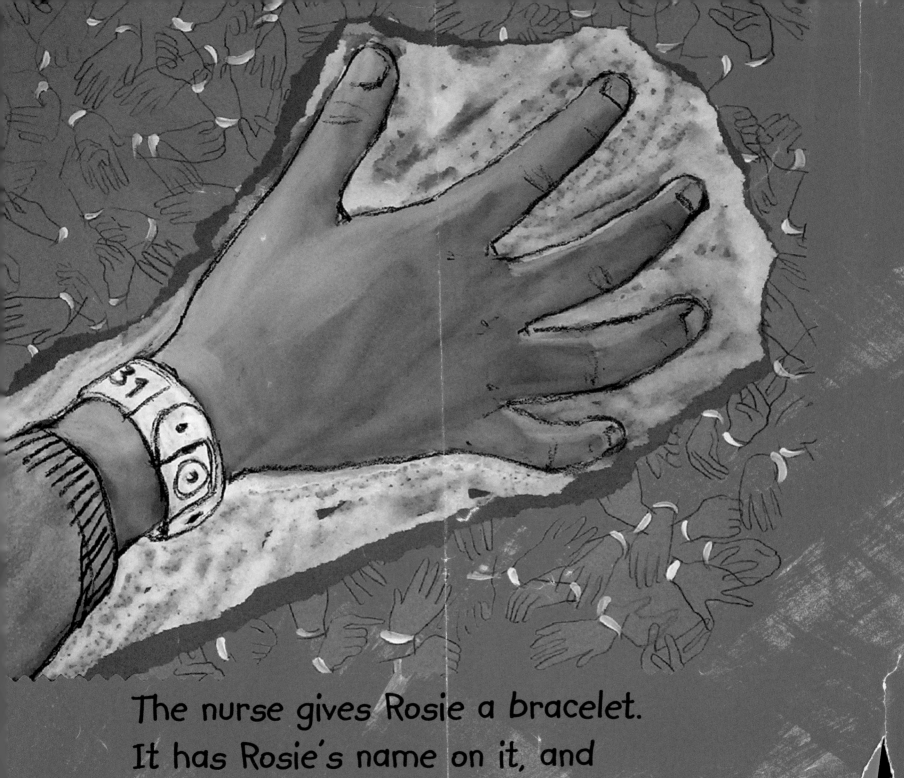

The nurse gives Rosie a bracelet.
It has Rosie's name on it, and
the number of her room.
Teddy gets a bracelet, too!

"Let me put your hair in pigtails," says Mom.
"Then it won't get tangled while you're asleep."
Rosie gives her mom a big hug.
"Don't worry, Mom," says Rosie.

"I'm going to give you an injection on your bottom," says the nurse.
"It will make you fall sound asleep. Then the operation won't hurt."

The nurse pushes Rosie's bed down the hall. Teddy enjoys the ride, but Rosie is falling asleep. The doctors get ready to make Rosie's heart better.

While Rosie is asleep, she can't feel anything. The doctors work hard to mend her heart. Teddy stays very close to her.

When Rosie wakes up, she feels dizzy.
Mom and Dad kiss her gently.
"You can come home soon," says Mom.
"But first you must rest in the hospital, and
take lots of medicines."

Rosie wakes up fully and looks at her chest.
What a big bandage!
Teddy has a bandage too, of course!

Rosie needs the bathroom, but
she has to stay in bed.
The nurse helps her to sit
on a funny pot called a bedpan.
It's metal, and feels cold on her bottom!

The nurse checks Rosie's blood pressure
and her temperature.
"You're doing well," says the nurse.
"Brave little girl."
The nurse checks three times a day.
What a lot of fuss!

Rosie starts to feel stronger.
The doctors come to see her.
"We're very proud of you, Rosie!
A star patient!"
Mom cries a bit — she is so happy that
Rosie is getting better.

Rosie has made a new friend
in the hospital, named Lucy.
They wave and call out to each other.

Rosie can get out of bed sometimes.
The scar on her chest still hurts a bit,
so she goes for a ride in a stroller.
Teddy goes too, of course.

Rosie doesn't feel very hungry
yet, even when Mom makes a
funny food face for her.

Every day, a lady checks Rosie's breathing. Rosie has to blow bubbles, lots of them.

It's hard to be brave all the time.
Sometimes at night Rosie cries.
She misses her dad, and her
brother and sister.
"Come in my bed for a hug," says Mom.

Rosie has lots of cards from her friends.
They help to cheer her up.

Rosie gets lots of visitors.
They bring her presents.
Rosie enjoys the fuss, but she
gets tired very quickly.

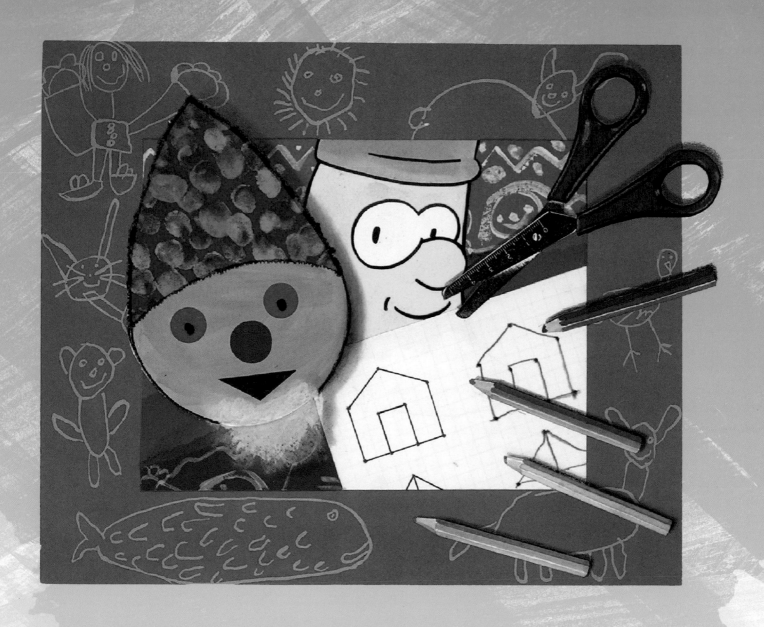

Now Rosie is well enough to go
to the hospital school.
She likes making pictures.

Rosie has her X-ray picture taken.

It shows her insides.

The doctors can check her heart and lungs.

Teddy takes a peek too.

"Time to take your bandage off,
Rosie," says the nurse.
"Blow out hard — that stops it from
hurting too much."
She takes Teddy's bandage off too.

Rosie's mom puts cream on her long scar.
"It will soon fade," she says.
Rosie's brother says,
"If the scar wasn't there, you
wouldn't be there either!"
And he's right.

"Let's listen to your heart," says the doctor. **Boom boom boom boom**, like a loud drum. "I think you can go home tomorrow," says the doctor.

Rosie packs her bag — so many
presents it will hardly shut.
At last, she's going home.
Mom has made a large chocolate cake,
even though it's not Rosie's birthday.